POSTCARD

Dear Reader,

My name is Edward Marshall Sr. I have four grandchildren. I call them Chillers, and they call me Grandude. I live in a very normal house on a very normal street, but when my Chillers come to stay, we go on adventures that are far from normal! Sometimes things get a little bit out of hand . . . but everything always works out fine in the end. Come and join us on an adventure!

Yours sincerely,

Grandude

Visit us on the Web! rhcbooks.com

Educators and librarians, for a variety of teaching tools, visit us at RHTeachersLibrarians.com

Library of Congress Cataloging-in-Publication Data is available upon request.
ISBN 978-0-525-64867-3 (trade) — ISBN 978-0-525-64868-0 (lib. bdg.) — ISBN 978-0-525-64869-7 (ebook)

Jacket art and interior illustrations by Kathryn Durst

MANUFACTURED IN CHINA
10 9 8 7 6 5 4 3 2 1
First American Edition

To every single one of my lovely family
—P.M.

For Annabella, Owen, and Charlotte. And for their amazing Grandude and Grandudette—my parents!
—K.D.

Hey Grandude!

Written by
Paul McCartney

Illustrated by
Kathryn Durst

Random House 🏠 New York

Lucy and Tom and Em and Bob were spending a weekend with their grandad.

Today was one of those days when nothing felt quite right.

Lucy

cookies

Tom

It was gray and drizzly, and everybody was grumpy and too bored to be bothered.

"Cheer up, Chillers!" said Grandude, and he pulled out a pile of postcards from the back pocket of his trousers.

"Look at these!"

Em

Bob

Em picked out a postcard of a sandy beach and sparkling blue waters.

"I wish we could go there, Grandude," she said.

"Well, let's see what we can do!"

Grandude reached into his coat pocket and took out a shiny compass.
He gave the compass a rub and waved it over the postcard.
The needle started to spin round and round. . . .

See the compass needle spin,
let the magic fun begin!

Then in a flash of magic . . .

Zing, bang, Sizzle ... everything changed!

The children were standing on a golden beach, with little waves tickling their toes. The water felt beautifully cool.

"We're on the beach from the postcard!" Bob laughed as he splashed in the sea.

But the magic compass hadn't finished yet! Huge flying fish leapt from the sea. "Hey, Grandude!" they called.

"It's a school of flying fish!" said Grandude. "Come on, Chillers— let's go for a ride!"

"A school?" whispered Lucy. "I hope we don't have to do any homework!"

They skimmed across shimmering blue waves on the backs of the flying fish, before coming to rest again on the hot sand.

They built sandcastles and then lay beneath a coconut tree, eating ice cream.

The memory of their gray, grumpy day was completely washed away, and they were perfectly happy . . .

until . . .

"Ouch!" cried Bob.

A little crab scuttled across the beach. "That crab pinched my toe!"

Oh no! Suddenly lots of little crabs were scurrying out of the sea, heading straight toward Grandude and the children!

"Hey, Grandude!" said Em. "Can we go somewhere a little less . . ."
"Pinchy! Yes, I think we'd better hop to it!" said Grandude.

He quickly waved the magic compass over another postcard.
This one had a picture of a cowboy.

See the compass needle spin,
let the magic fun begin!

The magic flashed and sparkled. And once again . . .

Zing, bang, Sizzle ... everything changed!

Grandude and the children found themselves
in a desert valley with spiky green cactuses.

A cowboy galloped toward them on a beautiful spotted horse.

"Hey, Grandude!" called the cowboy, waving his hat in the air.

"Wow, what a handsome Appaloosa!" said Grandude, admiring the horse.

"Appa-Lucy?" asked Em.

"No, that's the kind of horse it is— it has nothing to do with me!" said Lucy.

Grandude gave a whistle, and five more horses came galloping up. He helped each of the children onto a horse, and they raced together through the valley.

"Whee!" cried Bob.

"Faster!" yelled Lucy.

But what was that cloud
of dust on the horizon?

Oh no! A herd of wild buffalo was rushing straight toward them. The canyon echoed with the sound of a hundred hooves.

Before they could ride to safety, Tom's horse reared and he tumbled to the ground.

"Hold on, Tom!" shouted Grandude,
snatching a rope from the cowboy's saddle.

With a twirl, he lassoed Tom
and hauled him onto his horse.

"Ride, Chillers!" cried Grandude. "As fast as you can!"

They cleared the stampede—just in time!

"Hey, Grandude," panted Tom.
"Perhaps we could go somewhere
a little less . . ."

"Stampy! Yes, good idea!" said Grandude.
"And I think I need to cool down!"

Once again, he whipped out his magic compass
and waved it over a postcard.

See the compass needle spin,
let the magic fun begin!

Before the children could see the picture,
magic sparkled and flashed. And in the blink of an eye . . .

Zing, bang, Sizzle . . . everything changed!
They found themselves high on a hill in the afternoon sun.

The children laughed as they rolled in sweet-smelling wildflowers
that seemed to stretch forever. Grandude pulled out his trusty
guitar and began strumming a song.

"Hey, Grandude!" mooed
some friendly cows, their bells
tinkling along to the tune.

Grandude drew a small telescope from his pocket,
and they took turns looking at the snowcapped peaks.

But soon they heard a rumbling sound. . . .

Oh no!

"Hey, Grandude! Look!" yelled Lucy
as she peered through the telescope.

A huge wall of snow was sliding down
from the mountains above. . . .

AVALANCHE!

"Quick, Chillers!" cried Grandude.

"Jump!"

Just before the wave of snow reached them, Grandude and the children leapt onto one of the cows.

"Up, cow, up!" Grandude cried.

Magic swirled from the compass, lifting them all higher and higher off the ground . . .

. . . sailing them safely through the sky,
with the sea of snow rushing beneath them.

"Swiss cows are exceptionally
good fliers!" said Grandude.

Now, riding a flying cow is a lot of fun,
but it had been a very long day.

"Hey, Grandude!" said Lucy with a yawn.
"Maybe we could go somewhere a little more . . ."

"Sleepy!" said Grandude with a chuckle.
"That sounds like a very good idea!"

This time, instead of a postcard, Grandude pulled a photograph of his own house from his pocket.

Magic compass—one more spin, it's time for bedtime to begin!

He waved his compass over it, making the magic sparkle and spin.

And just like that . . .

Zing, bang, sizzle . . . they were back in Grandude's living room.

And the compass hadn't finished yet!

With a final flash of magic, the children were changed and ready for bed—their teeth were brushed, their faces were washed, and they were all tucked up tight.

And in five minutes flat, Tom and Bob and Lucy and Em
were fast asleep . . .

. . . dreaming of their next adventures!

*See the compass needle spin,
let the magic fun begin!*

Good night,
Grandude!